BABY GRIZZLY

Published in Canada by Fitzhenry & Whiteside, 195 Allstate Parkway, Markham, Ontario L3R 4T8
Published in the United States by Fitzhenry & Whiteside, 311 Washington Street, Brighton, Massachusetts 02135

www.fitzhenry.ca godwit@fitzhenry.ca

10 9 8 7 6 5 4 3 2 1

Library and Archives Canada Cataloguing in Publication
Baby grizzly / text by Aubrey Lang ; photography by Wayne Lynch.
(Nature babies series)
ISBN 1-55041-577-8 (bound) — ISBN 1-55041-579-4 (pbk.)

1. Grizzly bear—Infancy—Juvenile literature. 2. Bear cubs—Juvenile literature.
I. Lynch, Wayne II. Title. III. Series: Lang, Aubrey Nature babies series.

QL737.C27L355 2006   j599.784'139   C2005-907255-5

**U.S. Publisher Cataloging-in-Publication Data
(Library of Congress Standards)**
Lang, Aubrey.
Baby grizzly / text by Aubrey Lang ; photography by Wayne Lynch.
[36] p. : col. photos. ; cm. (Nature babies)
Includes index.
Summary: In Alaska, a mother grizzly cares for her three cubs. It will take more than a year
for the lively youngsters to grow and absorb their mother's lessons, which will ensure their future in the wild.
ISBN 1550415778 — ISBN 1550415794 (pbk.)

1. Grizzly bear – Infancy — Juvenile literature. 2. Bear cubs —
Juvenile literature. I. Lynch, Wayne. II. Title. III. Series.

Fitzhenry & Whiteside acknowledges with thanks the Canada Council for the Arts, and the Ontario Arts Council for their support of our publishing program. We acknowledge the financial support of the Government of Canada through the Book Publishing Industry Development Program (BPIDP) for our publishing activities.

Design by Wycliffe Smith Design Inc.
Printed in Hong Kong

BABY GRIZZLY

Text by Aubrey Lang
Photography by Wayne Lynch

Fitzhenry & Whiteside

BEFORE YOU BEGIN

Hello Young Reader:

We traveled to some wild areas in Alaska to write this book. We camped in a tent for many weeks, and spent the days watching mother grizzly bears and their cubs. We always stayed a safe distance from the bears so that we wouldn't disturb them. Sometimes the curious cubs would come very close; that always made us nervous because a mother bear is very protective of her young. To see what a bear sees when it goes fishing for salmon, we went snorkeling in the river.

We dedicate this book to our accomplished publisher Gail Winskill, who thought of producing the Nature Babies Series. Her vision and commitment to the project has greatly contributed to its success.

—Aubrey Lang and Wayne Lynch

TABLE OF CONTENTS

A new family of grizzly bears lives in Alaska, on a mountain slope covered with deep snow. The three tiny cubs were born one night during a fierce winter storm. The family of bears is safe and snug inside a den that the mother has dug under some willow bushes. Before the snow came, the mother grizzly gathered grasses and twigs to make a soft, dry bed for her babies. The bear family will stay inside the cozy den until the warm days of spring finally arrive.

It is May, and today the mother grizzly and her cubs will leave their winter den. The mother has not eaten for six months. She is very hungry. In the valley below, the snow has melted and there will be plenty of fresh, green grass for the mother to eat. The long trip down the mountain will be an adventure for the small cubs.

The growing cubs are always hungry. Every two or three hours, the mother stops to let them nurse. While the cubs suckle and slurp their mother's rich milk, Mama Grizzly looks around constantly. Big male bears can be dangerous for her cubs. After three days of travel, the tired family at last reaches the river that runs through the valley.

The mother leads the cubs to a meadow beside the river. Now it's her turn to eat. The two female cubs and their brother can barely see above the tall grass. They soon get bored and start munching like their mother. This is their first taste of green grass. By becoming copycats, they learn how to be grizzly bears.

13

Many hungry bears have also come to the valley to look for food. The other bears make the mother grizzly nervous. One day, while the family is walking beside the river, a big male bear chases after them. He almost catches the little male cub. The close call scares the mother, and she decides to take her family away from this dangerous place.

The mother grizzly heads toward the meadow where she was raised. The family will be safer there. The young cubs have to climb all the way back up the mountain. It's much more difficult to climb up a mountain than it is to come down. The cubs are still babies with short legs, and it takes the family more than a week to reach the safety of the meadow.

There is not much grass to eat in the meadow, so the mother grizzly must dig for food. The grizzly bear is a digging machine. She has long claws on her front feet and big, strong muscles that show up as a hump on her back. As she digs for juicy roots, the little male cub is often in her way. He is curious to see what she has found.

The mother likes the plant roots but they are small, and she needs plenty of them to fill her up. Every day, the mother grizzly spends many hours digging and digging. The cubs have lots of free time to play. The male cub likes to play the most. He wrestles and tumbles, and chases his sisters around. He even runs after feathers and leaves that blow across the ground.

Summer is over. It has started to snow again. Luckily the brother and his two sisters are healthy and strong. The cubs have made it through the most difficult time of their life. Their mother is nearby, digging a den so the family can spend the winter safely curled up together.

A year has passed. Now that the grizzly cubs are bigger, stronger, and faster, their mother can safely take them back to the river. Bears come to the river because it is a good place to fish for salmon. The salmon swim up the river to lay their eggs. The bears can easily catch the fish in shallow water.

There are many bears at the river today. When the river is crowded, bears often fight for the best fishing spots. The wise mother waits until some of the other bears leave. Her young male cub wants to follow her when she finally goes fishing, but he must stay on shore with his sisters. The mother grizzly soon returns with a big salmon.

Fishing looks easy to the young male. One day, while his mother and sister watch from shore, he decides to try it for himself. At first, he sticks his face underwater. It's a funny way to fish. Then he snorkels into deeper water. Even when a salmon bumps into his nose, the cub is not fast enough to catch it.

The young male cub and his sisters fatten up on salmon for the next couple of weeks. The mother grizzly may catch more than twenty-five salmon in one day. Because they

have so many fish to eat, the bears only eat the eggs and the skin—their favorite parts. Bald eagles also love salmon, and they often land nearby to feed on the leftovers.

This is the last summer the family will stay together. The young male grizzly and his sisters will spend one more winter in their mother's den. They will all separate next spring. The male cub will come back to the river every year to fatten up on salmon. One day, he may grow to be twice as big as his mother.

DID YOU KNOW?

- People often think that grizzlies and brown bears are different animals. They are really just different names for the same animal. They are also called the coastal brown bear, Alaskan brown bear, Kodiak bear, and silvertip grizzly.

- The size of an adult grizzly bear depends upon what it eats. Grizzlies that live in the inland mountains eat mainly roots, grass, berries, insects, and carrion (dead animals). The mountain grizzlies are often half as big as the grizzlies that live on the coast and feast on nutritious salmon. A big coastal male grizzly may weigh as much as 680 kilograms (1,500 pounds). If he stood on his hind legs, he would be over 2.5 meters (8 feet) tall.

- Grizzlies that live inland raise one or two cubs in a litter. Salmon-eating bears often give birth to three cubs, and sometimes even four.

- A grizzly bear could spend half its life hibernating in a den. There it lives off its thick layer of fat, losing one-quarter to one-third of its body weight over the winter.

- A grizzly cub is tiny at birth and weighs only 600 grams (21 oz). The little bruin is toothless; its eyes are sealed shut, and its body is covered with thin, short hair.

- The milk of a mother grizzly is very creamy. It contains 25% fat, compared to cow's milk, which contains just 4%. Newborn grizzly cubs nurse eight to ten times a day, and each session lasts less than ten minutes. As a cub gets older, it nurses less often. Some cubs may nurse until they are over two years old.

- Most grizzly bears in North America live in either Canada or Alaska. Only about one thousand grizzlies live in the lower forty-eight states, mainly in Glacier and Yellowstone National Parks.

INDEX

BIOGRAPHIES

When Dr. Wayne Lynch met Aubrey Lang, he was an emergency doctor and she was a pediatric nurse. Within five years they were married and had left their jobs in medicine to work together as writers and wildlife photographers. For twenty-seven years, they have explored the great wilderness areas of the world—tropical rainforests, remote islands in the Arctic and Antarctic, deserts, mountains, and African grasslands.

Dr. Lynch is a popular guest lecturer and an award-winning science writer. He is the author of over forty titles for adults and children. His books cover a wide range of subjects, from the biology and behavior of penguins and northern bears, arctic and grassland ecology, to the lives of prairie birds and mountain wildlife. He is a Fellow of the internationally recognized Explorers Club, and an elected Fellow of the prestigious Arctic Institute of North America.

Ms. Lang is the author of fourteen nature books for children. She loves to share her wildlife experiences with young readers.

The couple's impressive photo credits include thousands of images published worldwide.